Poptropica® FRIENDS

Quizzes and Activities for You, Your Friends & Your Life

by Tracey West

Poptropica

An Imprint of Penguin Group (USA) Inc.

D1308183

POPTROPICA

Published by the Penguin Group

Penguin Group (USA) Inc., 375 Hudson Street, New York, New York 10014, USA

USA | Canada | UK | Ireland | Australia | New Zealand | India | South Africa | China

Penguin Books Ltd, Registered Offices: 80 Strand, London WC2R ORL, England

For more information about the Penguin Group visit penguin.com

ISBN 978-0-448-46494-7   10 9 8 7 6 5 4 3 2 1

ALWAYS LEARNING   PEARSON

Goes the Quiz

If you've ever journeyed to the Islands of Poptropica, you've probably been asked a pop-quiz question. Even though these pop quizzes might be just a few words long, they can get you thinking about who you are as a person, or even about the people you know.

This book is full of pop quizzes and some other stuff, too—but don't worry, you won't get graded at the end. You don't even have to take the quizzes if you don't want to. You can use this book by yourself or share it with your friends.

If you're a by-the-book kind of person, you can start on the next page and go through all the pages in order. If you're more of a free spirit, you can open the book to a random page and start. And if you're not sure what kind of person you are, you'll probably find out after a few pages. That's the beauty of a pop quiz!

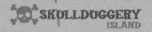

SKULLDUGGERY
ISLAND

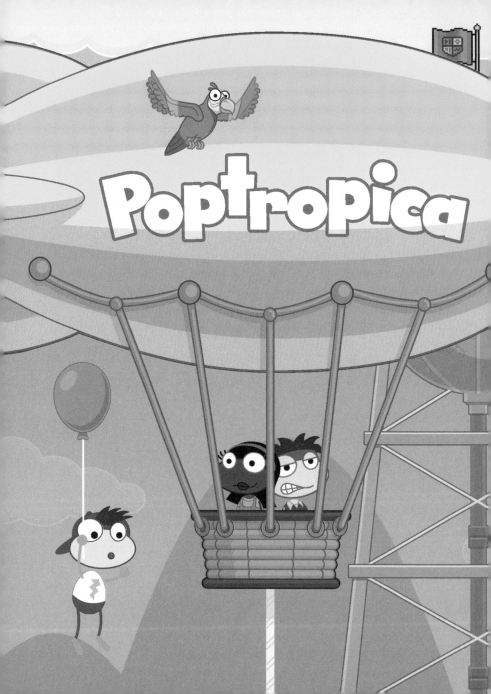

Table of Contents

POPTROPICA NAME GENERATOR

When you sign up for Poptropica, you're assigned a randomly generated name. In this book, you and your friends get to choose new names. Pick one from column A and one from column B.

Column A

Angry
Blue
Brave
Calm
Crazy
Dangerous
Dizzy
Golden
Hyper
Lone
Loud
Magic
Mighty
Sticky
Wild
Zippy

Column B

Axe
Beetle
Biker
Brain
Cactus
Carrot
Dragon
Hamburger
Knuckle
Ninja
Noodle
Owl
Shadow
Shark
Tomato
Wolf

Real Name: _____

Poptropica Name: _____

Real Name: _____

Poptropica Name: _____

Real Name: _____

Poptropica Name: _____

Real Name: _____

Poptropica Name: _____

Real Name: _____

Poptropica Name: _____

Real Name: _____

Poptropica Name: _____

Real Name: _____

Poptropica Name: _____

Real Name: _____

Poptropica Name: _____

Real Name: _____

Poptropica Name: _____

Real Name: _____

Poptropica Name: _____

Real Name: _____

Poptropica Name: _____

Real Name: _____

Poptropica Name: _____

Real Name: _____

Poptropica Name: _____

Real Name: _____

Poptropica Name: _____

Real Name: _____

Poptropica Name: _____

Real Name: _____

Poptropica Name: _____

Real Name: _____

Poptropica Name: _____

Who Are You?

In this section, you'll start to get to know yourself a little better. Who knows—some of your answers may surprise you.

STICK BADGE HERE. SECTION COMPLETED.

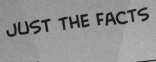

JUST THE FACTS

What's your name? _____

How tall are you? _____

What color is your hair? _____

What color are your eyes? _____

How many brothers or sisters do you have? _____

Where do you go to school? _____

What country do you live in? _____

OR ?

Do you like it ( ) or dislike it ( )?
Circle your answer.

Snow

Zombies

Mayonnaise

Loud music

Taking a shower

Broccoli

Classical music

Taking tests

Scary movies

Burned toast

Ants

Bubble baths

Candy that sticks to your teeth

Homework

Riding in the backseat

Going to the zoo

Hot sauce

Slippers

Sleeping late

Mice

Oatmeal

Roller coasters

Lime green

Baby powder

Cartoons

Thunderstorms

MORE ABOUT YOU

Check your answer.

	Yes	No
Would you eat candy for dinner?	☐ Yes	☐ No
Have you ever eaten sushi?	☐ Yes	☐ No
Do you wear glasses?	☐ Yes	☐ No
Have you ever given yourself a haircut?	☐ Yes	☐ No
Have you ever been in detention?	☐ Yes	☐ No
Have you ever broken a bone?	☐ Yes	☐ No
Have you ever accidentally used someone else's toothbrush?	☐ Yes	☐ No
Have you ever won a contest?	☐ Yes	☐ No
Have you ever been bitten by a dog?	☐ Yes	☐ No
Have you ever been in a fistfight?	☐ Yes	☐ No
Do you crack your knuckles?	☐ Yes	☐ No
Have you ever broken something that wasn't yours?	☐ Yes	☐ No
Do you bite your fingernails?	☐ Yes	☐ No
Do you sleep with a night-light?	☐ Yes	☐ No

Would you like someone to throw you
a surprise party?

Do you recycle? ☐ Yes ☐ No

Are you color-blind? ☐ Yes ☐ No

Have you ever faked sick to stay home
from school? ☐ Yes ☐ No

Can you keep a secret? ☐ Yes ☐ No

Do you have an imaginary friend? ☐ Yes ☐ No

Do you like to play practical jokes? ☐ Yes ☐ No

Have you ever baked a cake? ☐ Yes ☐ No

Do you have your own cell phone? ☐ Yes ☐ No

Do you share a bedroom? ☐ Yes ☐ No

Are you ticklish? ☐ Yes ☐ No

Do you have a short temper? ☐ Yes ☐ No

Do you know sign language? ☐ Yes ☐ No

Have you ever found money in the street? ☐ Yes ☐ No

EVEN MORE ABOUT YOU

Because sometimes, a yes or no answer just won't cut it.

Circle your answer.

What size dog do you like?

Small   Medium-size   Big

How do you get to school?

Bus   Car   Train   Walk

What's your favorite burger?

Hamburger   Cheeseburger   Veggie burger

What's your favorite season?

Summer   Fall   Winter   Spring

Do you live in the country or the city?

Country   City

Which pet would you rather have?

Dog   Cat   Bird   Fish   None

How do you prefer to talk to your friends?

In person   On the phone   Text   Webcam

Are you right-handed or left-handed?

Right-handed   Left-handed   Both

How clean is your room?

Spotless   A little messy   Pigsty

How many times a day do you brush your teeth?

0x   1x   2x   3x   4+

How do you like your ice cream?

Cone   Bowl

Are you a spender or a saver?

Spender   Saver

Do you sleep with a stuffed animal?

Yes   No   Yes, but don't tell anyone

What would you do with a million dollars?

Save it   Spend it   Give it to charity

What do you like on your pizza?

Cheese   Pepperoni   Veggies   Anchovies

What's Up with Your Friends?

How well do you really know your friends?
In this section, you can find out how you feel about
your friends. There are also some pop quizzes that
you can do with them. But first, let's figure out
who these people are.

STICK
BADGE
HERE.
SECTION
COMPLETED.

Who do you consider your best friend? _____

Which friend have you known the longest? _____

Who is your tallest friend? _____

Which friend looks the most like you? _____

Who lives closest to you? _____

Who has the most classes with you? _____

Which friend do you argue with the most? _____

Which friend do you wish was your brother or sister? _____

CREATE-A-FRIEND

What would your perfect friend be like? Circle one answer for each question to create the best friend of your dreams.

1. My best friend would . . .
    A. never forget my birthday.
    B. text me every day.
    C. give me my space.

2. I want a best friend who . . .
    A. makes me laugh.
    B. helps me with homework.
    C. goes running with me.

3. When we hang out, I want my best friend to . . .
    A. let me choose where we go.
    B. pick something for us to do.
    C. dress really nice, because style is everything.

4. I want a best friend who can . . .
   A. bake cookies for me.
   B. do impressions.
   C. drive.

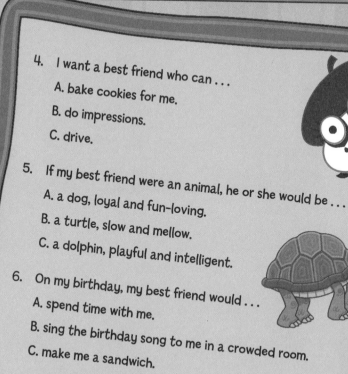

5. If my best friend were an animal, he or she would be . . .
   A. a dog, loyal and fun-loving.
   B. a turtle, slow and mellow.
   C. a dolphin, playful and intelligent.

6. On my birthday, my best friend would . . .
   A. spend time with me.
   B. sing the birthday song to me in a crowded room.
   C. make me a sandwich.

7. On a snow day, my best friend and I would . . .
   A. go sledding down the highest hill.
   B. stay inside and watch movies.
   C. text each other all day.

8. At school, my best friend and I would . . .
   A. wear matching outfits.
   B. sit together at lunch.
   C. help each other study.

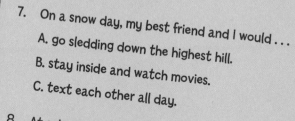

ONE WORD

Do any of these words describe your friends? Write the name of a friend who best fits the word.

WHICH OF YOUR FRIENDS IS . . . ?

Adventurous _____

Calm _____

Excitable _____

Cute _____

Sleepy _____

Ridiculous _____

Athletic _____

Studious _____

Helpful _____

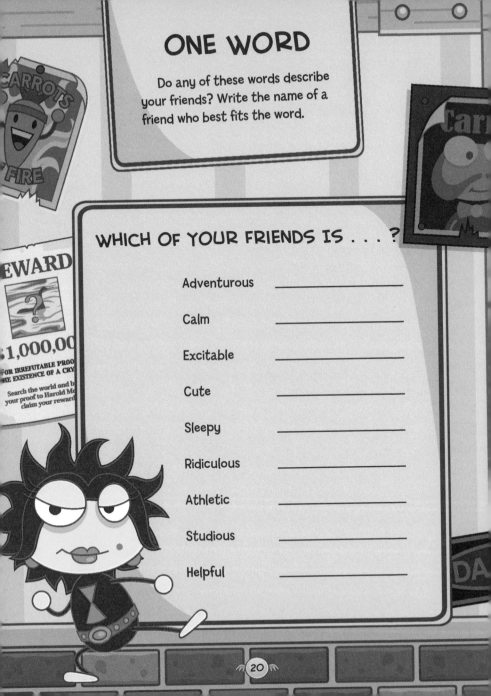

Loyal _____

Kind _____

Impatient _____

Stubborn _____

Funny _____

Clever _____

Creative _____

Sporty _____

Serious _____

Quiet _____

Outgoing _____

Chill _____

Hardworking _____

FLYING

MY FRIENDS SAY I'M . . .

What do your friends really think about you? Ask them to choose the word they think best describes you.

Smart

Fabulous

Interesting

Cute

Funny

Freaky

Generous

LOYAL

Lazy

Athletic

Weird

Mysterious

Crazy

Nice

FAST

Awesome

Awkward

Slow

Angry

Honest

AWESOME OR AWFUL?

Obviously, you and your friends like a lot of the same things, but nobody agrees on everything! Take this quiz together to find out what you've got in common—and what your friend is just plain wrong about.

Me

☐ Awesome ☐ Awful
☐ Awesome ☐ Awful
☐ Awesome ☐ Awful
☐ Awesome ☐ Awful
☐ Awesome ☐ Awful
☐ Awesome ☐ Awful
☐ Awesome ☐ Awful
☐ Awesome ☐ Awful
☐ Awesome ☐ Awful
☐ Awesome ☐ Awful
☐ Awesome ☐ Awful
☐ Awesome ☐ Awful
☐ Awesome ☐ Awful
☐ Awesome ☐ Awful

Sushi
Sad movies
Black licorice
Getting up early
Singing in the shower
Camping
Ketchup on eggs
Snakes
Boy bands
Pickles
Birthday-party hats
Long car rides
The color pink

My Friend

☐ Awesome ☐ Awful
☐ Awesome ☐ Awful
☐ Awesome ☐ Awful
☐ Awesome ☐ Awful
☐ Awesome ☐ Awful
☐ Awesome ☐ Awful
☐ Awesome ☐ Awful
☐ Awesome ☐ Awful
☐ Awesome ☐ Awful
☐ Awesome ☐ Awful
☐ Awesome ☐ Awful
☐ Awesome ☐ Awful
☐ Awesome ☐ Awful

FRENCH FRIES

Me

☐ Awesome ☐ Awful		
☐ Awesome ☐ Awful	Baseball	
☐ Awesome ☐ Awful	Stuffed animals	
☐ Awesome ☐ Awful	Staying up late	
☐ Awesome ☐ Awful	Gym class	
☐ Awesome ☐ Awful	Asparagus	
☐ Awesome ☐ Awful	Comic books	
☐ Awesome ☐ Awful	Halloween costumes	
☐ Awesome ☐ Awful	Thumb wars	
☐ Awesome ☐ Awful	Family reunions	
☐ Awesome ☐ Awful	Perfume	
☐ Awesome ☐ Awful	Little dogs	
☐ Awesome ☐ Awful	Ham-and-pineapple pizza	
☐ Awesome ☐ Awful	Being called on by the teacher	
☐ Awesome ☐ Awful	The color black	
☐ Awesome ☐ Awful	Football	
☐ Awesome ☐ Awful	Clowns	
☐ Awesome ☐ Awful	Shopping at the mall	
☐ Awesome ☐ Awful	Baby sitting	

My Friend

☐ Awesome ☐ Awful
☐ Awesome ☐ Awful
☐ Awesome ☐ Awful
☐ Awesome ☐ Awful
☐ Awesome ☐ Awful
☐ Awesome ☐ Awful
☐ Awesome ☐ Awful
☐ Awesome ☐ Awful
☐ Awesome ☐ Awful
☐ Awesome ☐ Awful
☐ Awesome ☐ Awful

☐ Awesome ☐ Awful

☐ Awesome ☐ Awful
☐ Awesome ☐ Awful
☐ Awesome ☐ Awful
☐ Awesome ☐ Awful
☐ Awesome ☐ Awful
☐ Awesome ☐ Awful

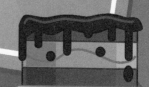

Free Time

You can tell a lot about a person by what they do in their free time. Do you like to relax, or are you always moving? When you have an extra hour to spare, do you do something fun, or organize your closet? (Or do you think organizing your closet is fun?)

Answer the pop quizzes in this section to find out what kind of free-time spender you are. But first, let's figure out what you like to do most.

STICK BADGE HERE. SECTION COMPLETED.

It's a Saturday afternoon. Your room is clean. You have no homework, no brothers or sisters to babysit, and no chores. You've got no dance practice or sports game to go to. So what do you do?

Think of ten things you like to do on a free day, and rate them here:

Most Awesome

1. _____
2. _____
3. _____
4. _____
5. _____
6. _____
7. _____
8. _____
9. _____
10. _____

Borderline Boring

POP QUIZ: RAINY DAYS

Answer these pop quizzes about stuff you do when there's nothing else going on.

Have you ever cried during a movie? ☐ Yes ☐ No

How well can you draw?   Well   Okay   Terribly

What's your favorite thing to do on a Saturday morning?

Sleep in   Watch cartoons   Play Poptropica

What's your favorite time of day?

Morning   Afternoon   Night

What's your favorite thing to do in Poptropica?   Play Island quests

Make friends   Battle other players   Get costumes

Have you ever made something with glitter? ☐ Yes ☐ No

What do you do on a rainy day?

Video game   Board game   Watch TV   Read

What TV show do you watch every time it comes on? _____

Do you sing in the rain? ☐ Yes ☐ No

What's your favorite day of the week? _____

What board game do you always win? _____

What board game do you always lose? _____

Can you perform any magic tricks? ☐ Yes ☐ No

What do you collect?

Stamps   Rocks   Action figures   Nothing   Other: _____

If you had an extra hour, how would you rather spend it?

Alone   With one friend   With lots of friends

Which is best?

Crayons   Markers   Colored pencils   Gel pens

What movie have you seen the most times? _____

What's the longest you've spent playing a video game without stopping?

1 hour or less   2-4 hours   4-6 hours   6 or more hours

What's the best kind of video game?

Action   Sports   Fantasy   Dance

Do you brush your hair before you video chat? ☐ Yes ☐ No

Do you keep a journal? ☐ Yes ☐ No

POP QUIZ: MUSIC

How does your taste in music mash up with other people in your life? Take this quiz with a friend and compare when you're done.

Me		My Friend
		My Friend
☐ Yes ☐ No	Do you play an instrument?	☐ Yes ☐ No
☐ Yes ☐ No	Have you ever sung in public?	☐ Yes ☐ No
☐ Yes ☐ No	Do you sing in the shower?	☐ Yes ☐ No
☐ Yes ☐ No	Have you ever sung along wearing your headphones and thought no one was listening, but someone was?	☐ Yes ☐ No
☐ Yes ☐ No	Are you in a marching band?	☐ Yes ☐ No
☐ Yes ☐ No	Have you ever formed a band with your friends?	☐ Yes ☐ No
☐ Yes ☐ No	Do you like country music?	☐ Yes ☐ No
☐ Yes ☐ No	Do you like rock music?	☐ Yes ☐ No
☐ Yes ☐ No	Do you like pop music?	☐ Yes ☐ No

Me

☐ Yes ☐ No

☐ Yes ☐ No

☐ Yes ☐ No

☐ Yes ☐ No

☐ Yes ☐ No

☐ Yes ☐ No

☐ Yes ☐ No

☐ Yes ☐ No

☐ Yes ☐ No

☐ Yes ☐ No

☐ Yes ☐ No

My Friend

Do you like punk rock?

Do you like disco music?

Have you ever played a kazoo?

Do you dream of auditioning for a singing-competition show?

Do your parents let you choose the radio station in the car?

Have you ever seen a Broadway musical?

Have you ever written a song?

Can you read music?

Did you ever go caroling?

Do you sing in a choir?

Do you like to dance?

☐ Yes ☐ No

☐ Yes ☐ No

☐ Yes ☐ No

☐ Yes ☐ No

☐ Yes ☐ No

☐ Yes ☐ No

☐ Yes ☐ No

☐ Yes ☐ No

☐ Yes ☐ No

☐ Yes ☐ No

☐ Yes ☐ No

THE Soothing Sounds

LET'S HANG OUT!

Every Island in Poptropica has one hangout where you can go and meet other Poptropicans. You can talk, battle them in mini-games, or just hang around.

These hangouts are known as common rooms. How many have you visited? Put a check next to each one. (And if you haven't visited some of them, go check them out and come back!)

- ☐ Arcade (Early Poptropica)
- ☐ Atlas Gym (Mythology Island)
- ☐ Bananabee's (Night Watch Island)
- ☐ The Barn (Vampire's Curse Island)
- ☐ B Cinema (Zomberry Island)
- ☐ Bert's Bed and Breakfast (Cryptids Island)
- ☐ Billiards Hall (Reality TV Island)
- ☐ Björn's Smorgasbord (Twisted Thicket)
- ☐ The Broken Barrel (Skullduggery Island)
- ☐ Cap'n Salty's (Big Nate Island)
- ☐ Celebrity Wax Museum (Back Lot Island)
- ☐ Cinema (24 Carrot Island)
- ☐ Coconut Café (Shark Tooth Island)
- ☐ Crop Circle Inn (Astro-Knights Island)
- ☐ Daggoo's Fish Market (S.O.S. Island)
- ☐ The Daily Paper (Super Power Island)

- ☐ The Dusty Gulch Hotel (Wild West Island)
- ☐ Final Frontier Gift Shop (Lunar Colony)
- ☐ Fly-by-Night Airlines (Nabooti Island)
- ☐ Flying Ace Café (Great Pumpkin Island)
- ☐ Frog Creek Library (Red Dragon Island)
- ☐ The Hair Club (Spy Island)
- ☐ Laser Tag (Wimpy Boardwalk)
- ☐ The Moldy Baguette Inn (Counterfeit Island)
- ☐ Party Time Tower (Time Tangled Island)
- ☐ Photo Gallery (Wimpy Wonderland)
- ☐ Poptropolis Training Hall and Gym (Poptropolis Games)
- ☐ Reverie Lounge (Mystery Train)
- ☐ Robo-Bling Boutique (Game Show Island)
- ☐ Soda Pop Shop (Early Poptropica)
- ☐ The Steamworks Gear Shop (Steamworks Island)
- ☐ Visitor Center (Ghost Story Island)
- ☐ You Know the Drill Eatery (Super Villain Island)

Which common room is your favorite?

_____

POP QUIZ: BOOKS

If you hate reading, you'll probably hate this pop quiz; but since you're reading a book now, the odds are good that you'll enjoy this. So give it a try.

Do you read books for fun? ☐ Yes ☐ No

What's the last book you read? _____

What's the first book ever you remember reading? _____

Have you ever stayed up all night to read a book?
☐ Yes ☐ No

Have you ever skipped to the last page to get to the ending?
☐ Yes ☐ No

Which do you use as a bookmark?

Folded-down page   Napkin   Actual bookmark

Which is the best genre?

Science fiction   Fantasy   Realistic fiction   Nonfiction   Historical fiction

Do you know how to use the Dewey decimal system?

☐ Yes ☐ No ☐ What's a Dewey decimal system?

Who's your favorite author? _____

Have you ever met an author in person? ☐ Yes ☐ No

Have you ever written a letter to an author? ☐ Yes ☐ No

Which would you rather do?

Read the book   Watch the movie based on the book

Which do you prefer?

Book made of paper   E-book

Where's the best place to read a book?

In bed   Under a tree   On the beach

Have you ever written a book? ☐ Yes ☐ No

What's your favorite book series? _____

What do you think of libraries?

Heaven on earth   Too quiet   Boring

Have you ever lost a library book?

☐ Yes ☐ No

Good vs. Evil

Nobody likes evil, but bad guys can be kind of fun, can't they? In this section, you'll take some pop quizzes about heroes and villains. But first, let's see how evil you are . . . *mwah-ha-ha!*

STICK BADGE HERE. SECTION COMPLETED.

Have You Ever . . .

1. . . . peeked at someone else's test paper? ☐ Yes ☐ No

2. . . . told your brother he was left on the doorstep by howler monkeys? ☐ Yes ☐ No

3. . . . cut in line? ☐ Yes ☐ No

4. . . . read a book under the covers while you're supposed to be sleeping? ☐ Yes ☐ No

5. . . . said you didn't do something, when you really did it? ☐ Yes ☐ No

6. . . . told a secret you weren't supposed to tell? ☐ Yes ☐ No

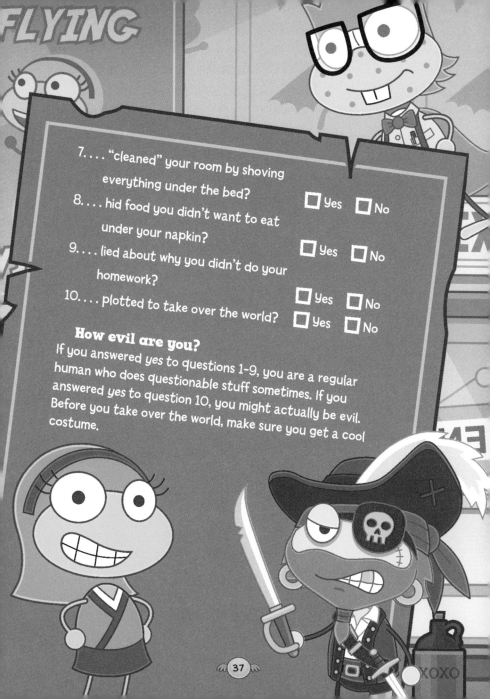

7. . . . "cleaned" your room by shoving everything under the bed?

☐ Yes ☐ No

8. . . . hid food you didn't want to eat under your napkin?

☐ Yes ☐ No

9. . . . lied about why you didn't do your homework?

☐ Yes ☐ No

10. . . . plotted to take over the world?

☐ Yes ☐ No

How evil are you?

If you answered *yes* to questions 1–9, you are a regular human who does questionable stuff sometimes. If you answered *yes* to question 10, you might actually be evil. Before you take over the world, make sure you get a cool costume.

BATTLING BAD GUYS

Poptropica is populated with villains, each more dastardly than the last. Some are evil geniuses, and some are just plain evil. It makes you wonder what would happen if these baddies were pitted against each other. Which Poptropica villain would win in a fight?

Dr. Hare versus
Mr. Silva

Speeding Spike versus
Crusher

Copy Cat versus
Sir Rebral

Director D. versus
Black Widow

Betty Jetty versus
Gretchen Grimlock

Zeus versus
Medusa

Captain Crawfish versus
El Mustachio Grande

 Binary Bard versus
Holmes

 Vince versus
_____

 Plant Monster versus
_____

 Mademoiselle Moreau
versus _____

 Count Bram versus
_____

Which of these villains do you think you could defeat?

_____

Which of these villains would you most like to hang out with?

_____

MOVIE TIME

Grab some popcorn and turn down the lights: It's time for a quiz about your favorite movie heroes and villains.

My favorite superhero movie of all time is:

_____

My favorite hero in the movie is:

_____

My favorite movie villain is:

_____

I wish they would make a movie about this superhero:

_____

The superhero movie sequel I can't wait to see is:

_____

POPCORN

POP CORN

B.A.D

WHO IS BETTER?
(CIRCLE YOUR CHOICE.)

Batman or Superman

Katniss Everdeen or Bella Swan

Spider-Man or Iron Man

Hermione Granger or Ron Weasley

Harry Potter or Draco Malfoy

The Hulk or The Thing

Woody or Buzz Lightyear

Luke Skywalker or Han Solo

Boba Fett or Darth Vader

Captain Kirk or Mr. Spock

Shrek or Puss in Boots

Phoenix or Storm

Doc Ock or The Sandman

Venom or Green Goblin

Rogue or Shadowcat

Wolverine or Cyclops

Joker or Catwoman

Princess Leia or Princess Amidala

Elizabeth Swann or Captain Jack Sparrow

Hawkeye or Black Widow

Thor or Loki

CREATE-A-COSTUME

Every superhero needs a costume. That outfit should either tell the world who you are, help you perform amazing heroic feats, or strike fear into the hearts of your enemies. What would your superhero costume look like? Circle one item for each part of your costume.

MASK

HAT

CAPE

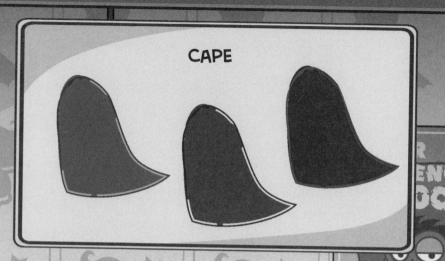

WEAPON

YOU'VE GOT THE POWER

Imagine that you could bestow a superpower on each of your friends. Fill in their names below to determine who gets what. (Make sure to give yourself a power, too!)

POWER	WHO GETS IT?
Flight	
Invisibility	
Superstrength	
Superspeed	
Mind reading	
Telekinesis (move stuff with your mind)	
Superior intelligence	
Control the weather	
Communicate with animals	
Walk through walls	
Teleportation	

Turn things to ice

_____

Control computers with mind power

_____

Stretch body like rubber

_____

Gills like a fish

_____

Transform into an animal

_____

Predict the future

_____

Shrink at will

_____

Become gigantic at will

_____

Speak in any language in the universe

_____

Travel back and forth in time

_____

Which superpower would you love
to have that's not on this list?

_____

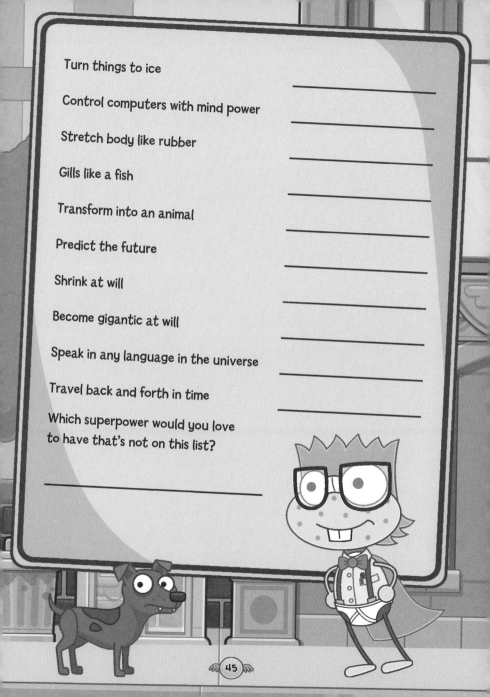

Ready, Set, Go!

Are you a sports nut or a couch potato?
Either way, you'll be pumped up about the quizzes
in this section! Head to the starting line and answer
a few questions to get started.

STICK
BADGE
HERE.
SECTION
COMPLETED.

Do you like to watch or play at least one sport?

☐ Yes ☐ No

If *yes*, continue to the next page.
If *no*, go immediately to page 48.

What is your favorite sport? _____

What is your favorite team? _____

Who is your favorite player? _____

If you play a sport, what position do you play?
_____

▽20m   ▽30m   ▽40m   ▽50m

WHO DOES IT BEST?

Have you ever been to Poptropica's Reality TV Island? There, you compete against seven other contestants to complete a series of challenges. Imagine that you and your friends are competing for the big prize. Which one of you would win?

CHALLENGE

WHO WOULD WIN?

Balanced Diet: balance food on a long, skinny pole

_____

Boulder Push: roll a boulder across a beach

_____

Coconut Catch: catch coconuts falling off a tree

_____

Hang Glider: glide through the sky and avoid obstacles

_____

Knockout: be the most accurate with a slingshot

_____

Geyser Guess: guess which geyser will explode first (no physical power necessary)

_____

On the Line: catch fish really fast

_____

Mountain Race: win a race up a steep mountainside

_____

Pole Climb: quickly climb to the top of a pole while avoiding falling coconuts

_____

Shot Put: throw a rock the farthest

_____

Shuffleboard: push your disc to the center of the target without being knocked away

_____

Totem Hop: keep your balance while standing on a shaking totem pole

_____

Water Run: avoid obstacles to fill a barrel from a waterfall

_____

POP QUIZ: SPORTS

Have you ever caught a foul ball at a game? ☐ Yes ☐ No

Have you ever ridden a horse? ☐ Yes ☐ No

Which is your favorite type of ball?

How high can you jump?   3 feet or less   3–5 feet   5 feet or more

Have you ever won a trophy for a sport? ☐ Yes ☐ No

How much weight can you lift?

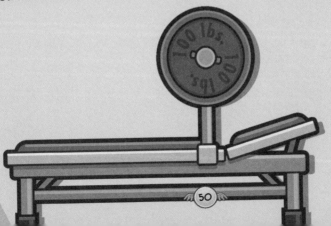

Do you know karate? ☐ Yes ☐ No

Do you do yoga? ☐ Yes ☐ No

Have you ever been injured by playing a sport? ☐ Yes ☐ No

Which is your favorite winter sport?
Ice-skating   Skiing   Snowboarding   Sitting by the fire

Have you ever hit a home run? ☐ Yes ☐ No

Do you bowl with the bumpers on or off? ☐ Yes ☐ No

Are you more likely to throw a strike in baseball or get a strike in bowling?
Baseball   Bowling

Can you run a mile without stopping? ☐ Yes ☐ No

Do you know how to swim? ☐ Yes ☐ No

Which is your favorite water sport?
Swimming   Waterskiing   Sailing   Diving

Which is your favorite backyard game?   Wiffle ball   Kickball   Volleyball

What happens when you put on ice skates?
Glide like a pro   Fall on my face

Have you ever won a game of mini golf? ☐ Yes ☐ No

Do you work out at a gym? ☐ Yes ☐ No

GYM CLASS QUIZZES

Whether or not you like sports, there's one place where everyone has to get moving: gym class. For some, it's fun; for others, it's a nightmare. What's your gym-class experience like?

What is your gym teacher's name? _____

Draw a dot to show where your gym teacher falls on the scale:

laid-back   sporty   extremely intense

Do you have to wear a gym uniform?

☐ Yes   ☐ No

Have you ever been chosen to be a team captain?

☐ Yes   ☐ No

Have you ever been picked last for a team?

☐ Yes   ☐ No

Have you ever faked being sick to get out of gym?

☐ Yes   ☐ No

How does dodgeball make you feel?   Excited   Indifferent   Terrified

What would you rather do than go to gym class?

Take a test   Get a cavity filled   Nothing, I love gym.

Where's the best place to have gym?

Inside   Outside   There is no best place to have gym.

Which team do you want to be on?   Red team   Blue team

Have you ever gotten a rope burn climbing the rope in   ☐ Yes   ☐ No
gym class?

Myths and Monsters

There are many places on Poptropica where you can find incredible creatures from stories and legends. In the forest of Twisted Thicket, you'll find creatures from Scandinavian mythology. On Mythology Island, you can talk to Greek gods and battle legendary monsters. On Cryptids Island, you'll search dark, faraway places for famous creatures. And on other Islands, you'll find dragons, robots, aliens, and more.

STICK BADGE HERE. SECTION COMPLETED.

ΣΤΟΑ T

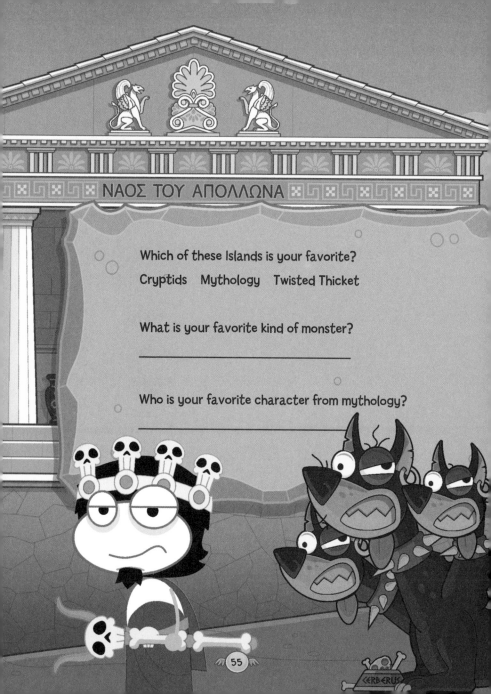

ΝΑΟΣ ΤΟΥ ΑΠΟΛΛΩΝΑ

Which of these Islands is your favorite?

Cryptids   Mythology   Twisted Thicket

What is your favorite kind of monster?

_____

Who is your favorite character from mythology?

_____

CERBERUS

WHICH IS SCARIER?

Circle the monster or creature that you wouldn't want to meet in a dark alley.

Dracula OR Frankenstein

Werewolf OR Vampire

Ghost OR Mummy

Alien OR Robot

Fast zombie OR Slow zombie

Ghoul OR Goblin

Cyclops OR Giant

Ogre OR Troll

Clown OR Mime

Kraken **OR** Hydra

Centipede **OR** Tarantula

50-foot woman **OR** 50-foot spider

Yeti **OR** Bigfoot

Chupacabra **OR** Jersey Devil

Can you think of a creature that's scarier than any of these?

_____

WANTED

CHUPACABRA

CAST YOUR FRIENDS

You're making a movie about the gods and goddesses of ancient Greece, and you need to cast your friends and family members in all of the roles. Who gets to play which part? Don't forget to cast yourself!

_____ starring as . . . Zeus, king of the gods

_____ starring as . . . Athena, goddess of wisdom

_____ starring as . . . Poseidon, god of the sea

_____ starring as . . . Aphrodite, goddess of love
                                              and beauty

_____ starring as . . . Hades, god of the underworld

_____ starring as . . . Apollo, god of music

_____ starring as . . . Artemis, goddess of wild animals

_____ starring as . . . Ares, god of war

_____ starring as . . . Hestia, goddess of the home

_____ starring as . . . Hercules, superstrong son of Zeus

_____ starring as . . . Medusa, snake-haired woman
                                              who turns people to stone

_____ starring as . . . Triton, Poseidon's surf-loving son

THE LEGEND OF THE CREATURE

Fill in the blanks to complete your own unique version of this mysterious tale. (Circle one of the words given, or use the prompts to come up with something on your own.) You can also have a friend come up with the words and then read the story out loud to them when you're done.

One dark night, Fierce Tomato was walking home from a friend's

house. A bright _____ shone overhead.
                    something in the night sky

"I think I'll take a shortcut," Fierce said, and she headed off

into the **forest/cemetery/empty lot**. As she walked, Fierce

thought she heard a/an _____ behind her.
                          soft sound

"Who's there?" Fierce asked, turning around. Then she thought

she saw something move in the shadows.

To her surprise, Fierce saw a glowing _____. The creature
                                        body part

let out a **howl/scream/wicked laugh**.

Heart pounding, Fierce resisted the urge to **run/scream/ cry like a baby**. What if this creature was something that nobody had ever seen before? She took out her cell phone, ready to snap a picture.

Then, without warning, the creature **lunged/jumped/flew** right at her! Its body was covered with **fur/feathers/scales**. **Sharp/Long/Huge** teeth filled its mouth, and two large **wings/horns/ears** grew from its back. Its breath smelled like

_____.
something that smells really bad

Frozen in fear, Fierce finally attempted to take the picture. But the creature swatted the phone out of her hands and then **ran/jumped/flew** away.

Terrified, Fierce ran to the main road. She couldn't wait to tell her friends—she had just encountered a real live _____!
name of creature

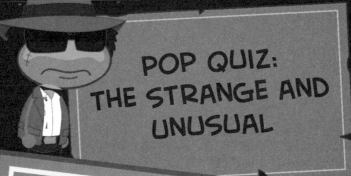

POP QUIZ: THE STRANGE AND UNUSUAL

Are you a fan of the weird, or are you happiest when things are normal?

Weird   Normal

Would you rather be locked in a room full of spiders or snakes?

Spiders   Snakes

Would you rather spend the night in a cemetery or a haunted house?

Cemetery   Haunted house

Have you ever seen a ghost?   ☐ Yes   ☐ No

Do you believe in Bigfoot?   ☐ Yes   ☐ No

Do you believe in ESP?   ☐ Yes   ☐ No

Do you believe in the Loch Ness monster?   ☐ Yes   ☐ No

Do you believe in UFOs?   ☐ Yes   ☐ No

Do you believe in ghosts?   ☐ Yes   ☐ No

Have you ever seen or heard something that you couldn't explain?

☐ Yes ☐ No

Do you think bad things happen on Friday the 13th?

☐ Yes ☐ No

Have you ever owned a black cat?

☐ Yes ☐ No

Would you rather be bitten by a vampire or a werewolf?

Vampire   Werewolf

Do you know anyone who was born on February 29?

☐ Yes ☐ No

Do you hold your breath when you pass by a cemetery?

☐ Yes ☐ No

Do you cross your fingers when you don't want to "jinx" something?

☐ Yes ☐ No

Which kind of Halloween costume do you like?

Scary   Cute   Funny   No costume

If you heard a strange noise at night, which would you do?

Go back to sleep   Get up and investigate

WHICH LEGENDARY CREATURE ARE YOU?

Answer each question, and then check the key at the end to find out.

1. Which of these is most important to you?

A. money

B. helping others

C. being outside

2. Where are you most comfortable?

A. underground

B. in the forest

C. in the sky

3. Which word or phrase best describes you?

A. hot-tempered

B. sweet

C. free spirit

4. Which of these colors are you most drawn to?

A. red and green

B. white and pink

C. purple and gold

5. Which kind of music do you like best?

A. rock

B. pop

C. classical

6. Which of these do you wish you could do?

A. breathe fire

B. run really fast

C. fly

7. Which of these seasons make you happiest?

A. winter

B. spring

C. summer

8. Which would you rather eat?

A. a big steak

B. a nice salad

C. spicy stir-fried rice

9. Which of these words appeals to you most?

A. comfort

B. innocence

C. freedom

10. Which country would you most like to visit?

A. Japan

B. Italy

C. Egypt

Which kind of legendary creature are you?

If you answered mostly As, you are a dragon. European dragons are vicious and greedy, and they hoard treasure. In Asia, dragons are helpful and symbolize good luck.

If you answered mostly Bs, you are a unicorn. This white horse, with the long horn spiraling from its forehead, is a symbol of purity, grace, and beauty.

If you answered mostly Cs, you are a phoenix. According to legend, when a phoenix dies, a new one rises from its ashes. The phoenix is associated with the sun and represents renewal.

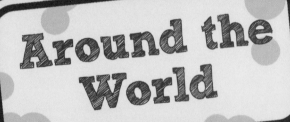

Around the World

Whether you love to explore the world or just around the block, you'll find pop quizzes in this section just for you.

STICK BADGE HERE. SECTION COMPLETED.

Which of these are true about you? (Check all that apply.)

- [ ] I wish I could travel all over the world.
- [ ] I'd like to visit every state in the United States.
- [ ] I'd rather not leave my house if I don't have to.
- [ ] I have my own set of luggage.
- [ ] I am terrified of flying on an airplane.
- [ ] I dream of going to a space station or the moon.
- [ ] My best vacations take place right where I live.
- [ ] I have been outside my state.
- [ ] I've never been outside my state, but I want to.
- [ ] I've never been outside my state, and that's just fine.
- [ ] My dream vehicle is an RV.
- [ ] I think long car trips are not boring at all.

TRAVEL QUIZZES

What kind of traveler are you?

Have you ever...

	Yes	No
...ridden on an airplane?	☐	☐
...ridden on a boat?	☐	☐
...ridden on a bus?	☐	☐
...ridden on a train?	☐	☐
...ridden in a hot-air balloon?	☐	☐
...lost your luggage?	☐	☐
...mailed someone a postcard?	☐	☐
...collected seashells?	☐	☐
...gotten carsick?	☐	☐
...slept outdoors?	☐	☐
...collected snow globes?	☐	☐
...eaten food you couldn't identify?	☐	☐

... gotten so lost that you had to turn back? ☐ Yes ☐ No

... visited another country? ☐ Yes ☐ No

... visited another state? ☐ Yes ☐ No

... visited another town? ☐ Yes ☐ No

... been stuck in an airport overnight? ☐ Yes ☐ No

... made a friend when you're on vacation? ☐ Yes ☐ No

... explored a forest? ☐ Yes ☐ No

... explored a jungle? ☐ Yes ☐ No

... explored a desert? ☐ Yes ☐ No

... explored a park? ☐ Yes ☐ No

... had a "staycation"? ☐ Yes ☐ No

... gotten a sunburn? ☐ Yes ☐ No

... gotten poison ivy? ☐ Yes ☐ No

... felt your ears pop? ☐ Yes ☐ No

... made an airport metal detector beep? ☐ Yes ☐ No

... ridden a horse? ☐ Yes ☐ No

... ridden on a roller coaster with a loop? ☐ Yes ☐ No

... gotten a suntan? ☐ Yes ☐ No

... climbed a mountain? ☐ Yes ☐ No

... gotten seasick? ☐ Yes ☐ No

YOUR DREAM JOURNEY

If you could go anywhere in the world and do anything in the world, what would it be? Pick a choice from each section to create your ideal trip of a lifetime.

I WANT TO . . .

Eat

Shop

Swim

Fish

Climb

Surf

Sail

Study

Explore

Relax

Skate

Run

Hike

Snowboard

Ski

Camp

See

Bike

Barbecue

Other: _____

IN/ON A/AN . . .

Mountain
Forest
Park
Museum
Backyard
Beach

Coral reef
Historic site
Ancient ruins
Mall
Open-air market
Restaurant
Big city

Small village
Wildlife preserve
Rain forest
Volcano
Island
Other: _____

IN . . .

China
Hawaii
California
France
Italy

Egypt
Japan
England
the United States
Canada
the Atlantic Ocean

the Pacific Ocean
the Arctic
the Antarctic
India
Other: _____

TRAVELOGUE

What are some interesting places you have visited? Use these pages to keep track.

Date: _____
I visited: _____
Rating: ☆ ☆ ☆ ☆ ☆

Date: _____
I visited: _____
Rating: ☆ ☆ ☆ ☆ ☆

Date: _____
I visited: _____
Rating: ☆ ☆ ☆ ☆ ☆

Date: _____
I visited: _____
Rating: ☆ ☆ ☆ ☆ ☆

Date: _____
I visited: _____
Rating: ☆ ☆ ☆ ☆ ☆

Date: _____
I visited: _____
Rating: ☆ ☆ ☆ ☆ ☆

Date: _____
I visited: _____
Rating: ☆ ☆ ☆ ☆ ☆

Date: _____
I visited: _____
Rating: ☆ ☆ ☆ ☆ ☆

Date: _____
I visited: _____
Rating: ☆ ☆ ☆ ☆ ☆

Date: _____
I visited: _____
Rating: ☆ ☆ ☆ ☆ ☆

Date: _____
I visited: _____
Rating: ☆ ☆ ☆ ☆ ☆

Date: _____
I visited: _____
Rating: ☆ ☆ ☆ ☆ ☆

Date: _____
I visited: _____
Rating: ☆ ☆ ☆ ☆ ☆

Date: _____
I visited: _____
Rating: ☆ ☆ ☆ ☆ ☆

Date: _____
I visited: _____
Rating: ☆ ☆ ☆ ☆ ☆

Date: _____
I visited: _____
Rating: ☆ ☆ ☆ ☆ ☆

Date: _____
I visited: _____
Rating: ☆ ☆ ☆ ☆ ☆

Date: _____
I visited: _____
Rating: ☆ ☆ ☆ ☆ ☆

PACK IT UP!

You're going away for the weekend, and you can only fit twelve things in your duffel bag. What will you bring?

CIRCLE YOUR CHOICES.

Toothbrush

Toothpaste

Soap

Shampoo

Deodorant

Body spray

Hair gel

Hair dryer

Socks

Underwear

Jeans

Shorts

T-shirt

Dress

Skirt

Sandals

Sneakers

Flip-flops

Snow boots

Hiking boots

Swimsuit

Towel

Sunscreen

Tennis racket

Snowboard

Book

Music player

Phone

Laptop

Winter coat

Gloves

Scarf

Floppy hat

Teddy bear

Journal and pen

Binoculars

Camera

Video camera

Night-vision goggles

Flashlight

Bug spray

Other:

_____

ISLAND ADVENTURER

Which Poptropica Islands have you visited? Give each one a rating from one to five (five is the highest). Put a check next to any Islands you've completed.

ISLAND	COMPLETED?	ISLAND RATING
24 Carrot Island	☐	☆ ☆ ☆ ☆ ☆
Astro-Knights Island	☐	☆ ☆ ☆ ☆ ☆
Back Lot Island	☐	☆ ☆ ☆ ☆ ☆
Big Nate Island	☐	☆ ☆ ☆ ☆ ☆
Charlie and the Chocolate Factory	☐	☆ ☆ ☆ ☆ ☆
Counterfeit Island	☐	☆ ☆ ☆ ☆ ☆
Cryptids Island	☐	☆ ☆ ☆ ☆ ☆
Early Poptropica	☐	☆ ☆ ☆ ☆ ☆
Game Show Island	☐	☆ ☆ ☆ ☆ ☆
Ghost Story Island	☐	☆ ☆ ☆ ☆ ☆
Great Pumpkin Island	☐	☆ ☆ ☆ ☆ ☆
Lunar Colony		

Mystery Train
Mythology Island
Nabooti Island
Night Watch Island
Poptropolis Games
Reality TV Island
Red Dragon Island
Shark Tooth Island
Shrink Ray Island
Skullduggery Island
S.O.S. Island
Spy Island
Steamworks Island
Super Power Island
Super Villain Island
Time Tangled Island
Twisted Thicket
Vampire's Curse Island
Wild West Island
Wimpy Boardwalk
Wimpy Wonderland
Zomberry Island

Tech Time

Is your dream to live in a world where you press a button to do everything, or are you longing to escape technology and go live off the grid? In this section, find out if you're a techno-freak or a technophobe.

STICK BADGE HERE. SECTION COMPLETED.

Would you rather own a tablet or a smartphone?

_____

Do you have good friends whom you've never met in person?
☐ Yes ☐ No

What's the one device you couldn't live without?

_____

How long have you been playing Poptropica?

A week   A month   A year   More than a year

What's your home page? _____

What search engine do you use most? _____

Technology makes life better.   True   False

I wish we could go back to a simpler time before
technology existed.   True   False

WHICH INVENTION IS BETTER?

Which of the inventions in each pair would you be unable to live without? Circle your choice.

Cell phone **OR** Television

Tablet **OR** Laptop

Electric toothbrush **OR** Electric blanket

Coffeemaker **OR** Toaster

Litter box **OR** Doggie bed

Computer **OR** Telephone

Calculator **OR** Bathroom scale

Alarm clock **OR** Doorbell

Smoke detector **OR** Fire extinguisher

Toaster oven **OR** Microwave

Chainsaw **OR** Electric drill

Bicycle **OR** Car

Stapler **OR** Tape dispenser

Radio **OR** Digital music player

Skateboard **OR** Scooter

Space heater **OR** Air conditioner

Printer **OR** Scanner

Earbuds **OR** Headphones

Electric guitar **OR** Computerized drum kit

Blow-dryer **OR** Curling iron

Hair gel **OR** Toothpaste

ROBOT QUIZZES

You don't have to go far on Poptropica before you bump into a robot or two. They run the gamut from friendly to fierce:

Merlin (Astro-Knights Island)
This robot owl will do your bidding if you keep him well fed.

Sprocket (Steamworks Island)
This friendly sidekick robot will follow you anywhere—even into danger.

The Bouncer (Game Show Island)
He keeps the riffraff out of Club Nouveau Riche and looks good doing it.

The Club Owner (Game Show Island)
This guy knows how to throw a party.

Training Robot (Night Watch Island)
He'll keep you on your toes for those late-night work shifts.

Holmes (Game Show Island)
This supercomputer is a genius—so he's evil, of course.

Mecha Mordred (Astro-Knights Island)
Part human, part robot, all bad.

Which robot would you want as a pet? _____

Which robot would you want to hang out with? _____

Which robot do you think is the most powerful? _____

Which robots have you defeated? _____

Which robot was hardest to defeat? _____

Are there any other Poptropica robots that you like? _____,

_____, _____, _____

POP QUIZ: TECHNOLOGY

Has your hard drive ever crashed? ☐ Yes ☐ No

Have you ever fixed someone's computer? ☐ Yes ☐ No

Have you ever sent an embarrassing text to the wrong person? ☐ Yes ☐ No

Do you use a laptop in school? ☐ Yes ☐ No

Have you ever lost your cell phone? ☐ Yes ☐ No

Have you lost your cell phone more than once? ☐ Yes ☐ No

Do you prefer to read books on a tablet? ☐ Yes ☐ No

Do you get all your music digitally? ☐ Yes ☐ No

FUSION
Y

Have you ever dropped your device in the toilet? ☐ Yes ☐ No

If you did, did you fish it out? ☐ Yes ☐ No

Did your cell phone ever go through the wash? ☐ Yes ☐ No

Have you ever cracked the screen of your device? ☐ Yes ☐ No

Has autocorrect ever caused you to send
out an embarrassing text?

Do you think cat memes are awesome? ☐ Yes ☐ No

Do you Skype? ☐ Yes ☐ No

Have you ever had your cell phone confiscated? ☐ Yes ☐ No

Have you ever spilled soda on your keyboard? ☐ Yes ☐ No

Do you own more than one handheld device? ☐ Yes ☐ No

Could you go 24 hours without texting? ☐ Yes ☐ No

Have you ever been in a viral video? ☐ Yes ☐ No

Phone

You've Got Style

Whether you read every fashion magazine from cover to cover or grab your clothes from the floor in the morning, you've got a sense of style that's uniquely yours.

STICK BADGE HERE. SECTION COMPLETED.

What are you wearing right now? _____

What's your favorite item of clothing? _____

Which word best describes your fashion sense?

Chic

Casual

Sporty

Bold

Bohemian

Stylish

Hip-hop

Dressy

Unique

Grunge

FUNKY

POP QUIZ: CLOTHES

Have you ever worn two different socks? ☐ Yes ☐ No

Have you ever worn two different shoes? ☐ Yes ☐ No

Have you ever gone out in public with your clothes on backward by mistake? ☐ Yes ☐ No

Do you wear pajama pants to school? ☐ Yes ☐ No

Have you ever worn the same pair of underwear two days in a row? ☐ Yes ☐ No

Do you do your own laundry? ☐ Yes ☐ No

Do you have to wear a uniform for gym class? ☐ Yes ☐ No

Do you own a T-shirt with your favorite band on it? ☐ Yes ☐ No

Do you own clothing with a sports-team logo? ☐ Yes ☐ No

Do you love getting clothes as presents? ☐ Yes ☐ No

Do you wear your sibling's hand-me-downs? ☐ Yes ☐ No

Have you ever worn jeans with holes in them? ☐ Yes ☐ No

Do you wear shorts even when it's cold out? ☐ Yes ☐ No

Have you ever worn a tuxedo? ☐ Yes ☐ No

Do you make your own clothes? ☐ Yes ☐ No

Do you subscribe to a fashion magazine? ☐ Yes ☐ No

Do you wear a hat indoors? ☐ Yes ☐ No

Have you ever worn sunglasses at night? ☐ Yes ☐ No

Would you wear fur? ☐ Yes ☐ No

Do you have swag? ☐ Yes ☐ No

COSTUME FACE-OFF

Which Poptropica costume is better?

IN OR OUT?

Which of these styles do you wear (or wish you wore), and which do you wish would disappear? See if your friends share your fashion sense!

Me

☐ In ☐ Out   Flip-flops

☐ In ☐ Out   Trucker caps

☐ In ☐ Out   Overalls

☐ In ☐ Out   Skinny jeans

☐ In ☐ Out   Scarves

☐ In ☐ Out   Cowboy boots

☐ In ☐ Out   Cowboy hats

☐ In ☐ Out   Leather jackets

☐ In ☐ Out   High-tops

☐ In ☐ Out   Hoodies

☐ In ☐ Out   Fedoras

☐ In ☐ Out   Ugg boots

☐ In ☐ Out   Sunglasses

☐ In ☐ Out   Football jerseys

My Friend

☐ In ☐ Out

☐ In ☐ Out

☐ In ☐ Out

☐ In ☐ Out

☐ In ☐ Out

☐ In ☐ Out

☐ In ☐ Out

☐ In ☐ Out

☐ In ☐ Out

☐ In ☐ Out

☐ In ☐ Out

☐ In ☐ Out

☐ In ☐ Out

☐ In ☐ Out

Me

☐ In ☐ Out

☐ In ☐ Out

☐ In ☐ Out

☐ In ☐ Out

☐ In ☐ Out

☐ In ☐ Out

☐ In ☐ Out

☐ In ☐ Out

☐ In ☐ Out

☐ In ☐ Out

☐ In ☐ Out

☐ In ☐ Out

☐ In ☐ Out

☐ In ☐ Out

☐ In ☐ Out

☐ In ☐ Out

☐ In ☐ Out

☐ In ☐ Out

My Friend

☐ In ☐ Out

☐ In ☐ Out

☐ In ☐ Out

☐ In ☐ Out

☐ In ☐ Out

☐ In ☐ Out

☐ In ☐ Out

☐ In ☐ Out

☐ In ☐ Out

☐ In ☐ Out

☐ In ☐ Out

☐ In ☐ Out

☐ In ☐ Out

☐ In ☐ Out

☐ In ☐ Out

☐ In ☐ Out

☐ In ☐ Out

☐ In ☐ Out

Flannel shirts

Sequins

T-shirts with funny sayings

Camouflage pants

Bow ties

Baggy jeans

Plaid shirts

Denim jackets

Vests

Ankle bracelets

Anything with feathers

Anything with fur

Knit caps

Footie pajamas

Knee socks

Belts

Friendship bracelets

Turtlenecks

POP STYLE

Every Island in Poptropica has its own style. Check out these Poptropica inhabitants. Which of these outfits do you wish you could own? Give each one a rating from ☆ to ☆ ☆ ☆ ☆ ☆.

☆ ☆ ☆ ☆ ☆   ☆ ☆ ☆ ☆ ☆   ☆ ☆ ☆ ☆ ☆   ☆ ☆ ☆ ☆ ☆

☆ ☆ ☆ ☆ ☆   ☆ ☆ ☆ ☆ ☆   ☆ ☆ ☆ ☆ ☆   ☆ ☆ ☆ ☆ ☆

☆ ☆ ☆ ☆ ☆   ☆ ☆ ☆ ☆ ☆   ☆ ☆ ☆ ☆ ☆   ☆ ☆ ☆ ☆ ☆

☆ ☆ ☆ ☆ ☆   ☆ ☆ ☆ ☆ ☆   ☆ ☆ ☆ ☆ ☆   ☆ ☆ ☆ ☆ ☆

☆ ☆ ☆ ☆ ☆   ☆ ☆ ☆ ☆ ☆   ☆ ☆ ☆ ☆ ☆   ☆ ☆ ☆ ☆ ☆

Move It!

Are you happiest when you're taking a hike, or do you dream of speeding down the highway or soaring through the clouds? The way you get from point A to point B can say a lot about your personality.

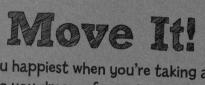

STICK BADGE HERE. SECTION COMPLETED.

Which ride suits you and your friends best? Assign a vehicle to each of your friends (and don't forget to pick one for yourself!).

Mountain bike _____

Motorcycle _____

All-terrain vehicle _____

Sports car _____

Smart car _____

Off-road vehicle _____

Van _____

Tour bus _____

RV _____

POP QUIZ: WHEELS

Have you ever popped a wheelie on a bike? ☐ Yes ☐ No

Have you ever wiped out on a skateboard? ☐ Yes ☐ No

Have you ever ridden a unicycle? ☐ Yes ☐ No

Which is the best bicycle accessory?　Basket　Bell　Headlight

How old were you when you learned to ride
   a two-wheeled bicycle? _____

Have you ever been a passenger on a motorcycle? ☐ Yes ☐ No

Do you own sneakers with wheels in them? ☐ Yes ☐ No

Which one is more fun?　Skateboard　Scooter

Have you ever seen a monster truck up close? ☐ Yes ☐ No

When a truck passes you on the highway, do
   you try to get the driver to beep his horn? ☐ Yes ☐ No

98

When you're in the family car, where do you sit?

Front passenger seat   Back left   Back middle   Back right

How often do you ride a bus?

Almost every day   Weekends   Sometimes   Never

Which type of skateboard is best?

Short board   Long board   No board

☐ Yes ☐ No

Do you have inline skates?

☐ Yes ☐ No

Have you ever ridden a Segway?

☐ Yes ☐ No

Have you ever ridden a bicycle built for two?

☐ Yes ☐ No

Have you ever ridden on a golf cart?

Which kind of vehicle is best?

A safe one   A fast one   One that's good for the environment

Which is the best accessory for a car?

Flames on side   Tree-shaped air freshener   Spinning hubcaps

BIG ZEKE'S

POP MY RIDE

When you explore Poptropica, you'll be able to get into the driver's seat of just about every kind of vehicle you can imagine. Which of these rides would you choose if you had a chance?

Jetpack **OR** Hovercraft

Pirate ship **OR** Rocket ship

Horse **OR** Pegasus

Giant Rabbot **OR** Mordred's Mecha robot fighting suit

Plane **OR** Helicopter

Jeep **OR** Kitesurfer X250

S.S. Pequod **OR** John Bull Locomotive

Excalibur spaceship **OR** PASE rocket ship

Dorf Bean car **OR** Scooter

Balloon **OR** Blimp

Golf cart **OR** Motorized scooter

BLING-OUT BLIMP

The flying yellow blimp has become the symbol of Poptropica. Imagine if you could customize your blimp before you took to the Poptropica skies. Use your imagination to give this blimp some personality.

FLYING
HIGH

SORE
LOSERS
NEVER SOAR

REWARD

$1,000,000

FOR IRREFUTABLE PROOF OF
THE EXISTENCE OF A CRYPTID.

Search the world and bring
your proof to Harold Mews to
claim your reward.

Po

Time Traveling

As many visitors to Poptropica know, it's possible to travel back to the past, or far into the future, depending on which Island you explore. So what kind of time traveler are you?

STICK BADGE HERE. SECTION COMPLETED.

Would you rather travel to the past or the future? _____

If you went back in time, which modern invention would you miss most? _____

Which period in history would you most want to visit?

_____

Which period in history do you think would be most dangerous?

_____

Which of your friends would be good time-travel companions?

_____ , _____ , _____

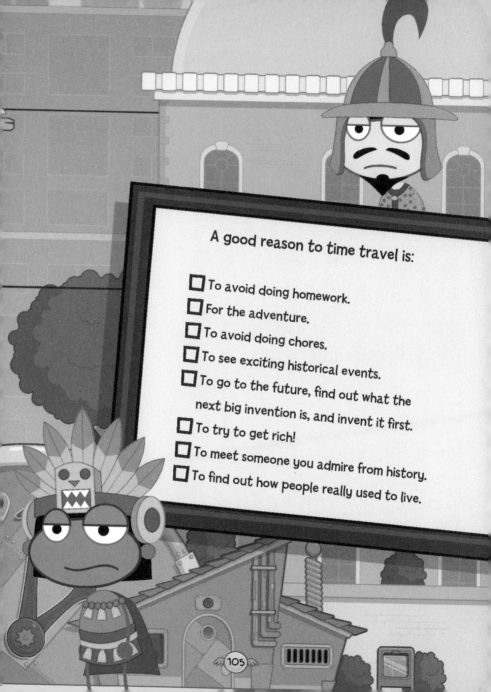

A good reason to time travel is:

☐ To avoid doing homework.
☐ For the adventure.
☐ To avoid doing chores.
☐ To see exciting historical events.
☐ To go to the future, find out what the next big invention is, and invent it first.
☐ To try to get rich!
☐ To meet someone you admire from history.
☐ To find out how people really used to live.

CHOOSE YOUR TIME!

Which time period would you want to visit—and what would you do when you got there?

Prehistoric

- ☐ Ride a stegosaurus
- ☐ Count how many teeth a T. rex has
- ☐ Fly on a pterodactyl
- ☐ Make a dinosaur-egg omelet

Ancient Egypt

- ☐ Become pharaoh
- ☐ Rob a tomb
- ☐ Get chased by a mummy
- ☐ Visit the pyramids

Renaissance England

- [ ] Learn to joust
- [ ] Help Shakespeare write a play
- [ ] Become a court jester
- [ ] Hang out with Queen Elizabeth I

Future

- [ ] Visit Earth's moon colony
- [ ] Take over the world with a robot army
- [ ] Pilot a spaceship
- [ ] Fly around with a jetpack

WHAT'S YOUR TIME-TRAVELER PERSONALITY?

If you and your friends could travel through space and time, who would best blend in where? Match up each picture to you and your friends!

LAB

Hunter—easily can survive in the wild; eats with hands.

_____
your name or friend's name

Pirate—"borrows" stuff from friends all the time; can go months without taking a shower.

_____
your name or friend's name

Astronaut—enjoys exploring strange new worlds; hates gravity.

_____
your name or friend's name

Old West sheriff—likes to lay down the law and tell people what to do.

_____
your name or friend's name

Viking—a lifetime of conquering foes, from the sandbox to the cafeteria.

_____
your name or friend's name

Queen or king—all smiles until you screw up, then it's off with your head!

_____
your name or friend's name

Temple designer—great friend to have around when you're playing with Legos.

_____
your name or friend's name

Gladiator—all-around tough guy and always looking for a fight.

_____
your name or friend's name

Robot scientist—we always knew all that tinkering with gadgets would pay off.

_____
your name or friend's name

Court jester—when you're this funny, who needs the silly hat?

_____
your name or friend's name

TOUGH TIME-TRAVELING CHOICES

When you're time traveling, you've got to be ready for anything. Which would you rather do? Circle your choice.

Mummify a body by taking its brains out through its nostrils
or
Become a human flytrap by slathering honey all over your body

Use a public toilet with no stalls
or
Brush your teeth with a toothbrush made out of pig hair and bone

Sleep on a pillow made of stone
or
Wear a wig made from itchy wool

Eat stale, dry crackers covered in bugs
or
Eat a pudding made from pigs' blood

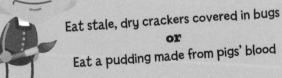

Heal a toothache by holding a dead mouse on your gums

or

Heal a toothache by eating a powder made from ground-up mummies

Sleep next to someone who hasn't washed or changed their clothes in over a year

or

Walk barefoot through streets covered with sewage from people and animals

Wear dentures made from the teeth of dead people

or

Wear dentures made from the teeth of dead animals

Pluck all the hair from your body, even your eyebrows and eyelashes

or

Dye your entire body blue from head to toe

Try to escape from an angry T. rex

or

Try to outrun a herd of stampeding triceratops

Go to a school where they make you steal your lunch, but if you're caught doing it, you are whipped

or

Go to school seven days a week from sunup till sundown

Back to Nature

Does the term *back to nature* make your skin crawl, or do you love the feel of grass under your bare feet? Take this quiz to see what kind of nature lover you are.

STICK
BADGE
HERE.
SECTION
COMPLETED.

1. My favorite place to see wild animals is
   A. on TV.
   B. up close.

2. The best part about a snow day is
   A. hot chocolate.
   B. going sledding.

3. The best way to sleep is
   A. in a comfy king-size bed.
   B. in a sleeping bag under the stars.

4. The best vegetables come from
   A. a five-star chef.
   B. my garden.

5. The best part about a day at the beach is
   A. going to the arcade at night.
   B. bodysurfing on the waves.

6. The best kind of walk is
   A. a walk around the mall.
   B. a walk around the park.

7. I think the desert is
   A. way too hot.
   B. a beautiful place to visit.

8. In my backpack you'll find
   A. my tablet, my cell phone, and my laptop.
   B. sunscreen, bug spray, and a water bottle.

If you answered mostly As . . . then your idea of experiencing nature is watching funny animal videos.

If you answered mostly Bs . . . then you are a true nature lover. Don't forget to slather on the sunscreen!

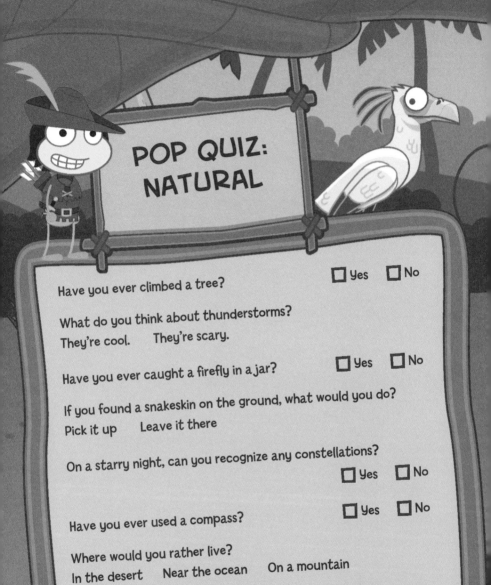

POP QUIZ: NATURAL

Have you ever climbed a tree? ☐ Yes ☐ No

What do you think about thunderstorms?
They're cool.   They're scary.

Have you ever caught a firefly in a jar? ☐ Yes ☐ No

If you found a snakeskin on the ground, what would you do?
Pick it up   Leave it there

On a starry night, can you recognize any constellations?
☐ Yes ☐ No

Have you ever used a compass? ☐ Yes ☐ No

Where would you rather live?
In the desert   Near the ocean   On a mountain

Have you ever been inside a cave? ☐ Yes ☐ No

Have you ever been bitten by a spider? ☐ Yes ☐ No

Have you ever planted a seed?

☐ Yes ☐ No

Which do you like best?
River   Lake   Ocean   Swimming pool

What do you do when you see a bee?
Run and scream   Remain calm   Watch to see where it goes

What's the best thing about spring?
Blooming flowers   Start of baseball season   Baby animals are born

What's the best thing about summer?
No school   Swimming   Camping

What's the best thing about fall?
Changing leaves   School starts   Football and soccer games

What's the best thing about winter?
Snow   Winter holidays   Winter sports

What do you think of rain?
It makes the plants grow.   It's boring.   I like to splash in puddles.

I WAS GOING FOR A HIKE . . .

You'll need some friends for this. Imagine you are going on a hike. The story starts below. Write the next line, and then give it to a friend to write the next one. (Pass it back and forth until the story's done.)

I was going for a hike one morning when I saw . . .

_____

_____

_____

_____

_____

_____

_____

_____

_____

THE END

Idea: Start your story somewhere in Poptropica, like the Twisted
Thicket or the Jungle Planet on Astro-Knights Island.

For Serious Poptropicans Only

Sure, we've quizzed you about Poptropica in this book, but these quizzes are for serious fans. What kind of fan are you?

> STICK BADGE HERE. SECTION COMPLETED.

How many Poptropica accounts do you have?

_____

What are your Poptropica names? _____

_____ , _____

How many hours a week are you on Poptropica?

1–3   3–7   7 or more

Have you ever stayed up all night trying to finish an Island? Yes ☐ No

Do you dream about Poptropica? ☐ Yes ☐ No

Do you own a pet named after a
   Poptropica character? ☐ Yes ☐ No

Have you visited a Poptropica fan site? ☐ Yes ☐ No

Have you read the *Poptropica Official Guide*
   from cover to cover? ☐ Yes ☐ No

What is your favorite Poptropica Island? _____

YOUR ULTIMATE GOLD CARD

In Poptropica, you can get Gold Cards to enhance your character. A Gold Card might contain an item that you can use in a game for fun, like fireworks, or allow you to change your appearance, or temporarily give you special powers.

What Gold Card would you create? Describe your ultimate Gold Card below, and draw a picture of it on the next page.

Gold Card Name: _____

What It Does: _____

_____

_____

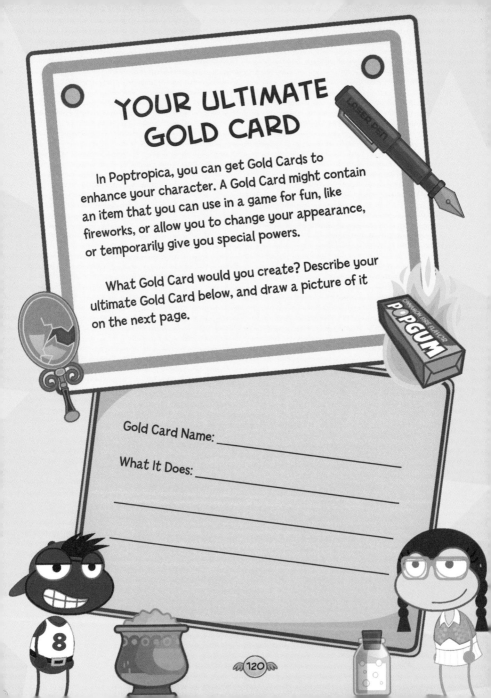

YOUR DREAM ISLAND

What if you could combine characters and places from your favorite Islands to create something just for you?

Pick one good guy:

☐ Professor Hammerhead

☐ Annie Oakley

☐ Athena

☐ CJ

☐ Ned Noodlehead

☐ Other: _____

Pick one villain:

☐ El Mustachio Grande

☐ Dr. Hare

☐ Black Widow

☐ Captain Crawfish

☐ Mademoiselle Moreau

☐ Other: _____

Pick two creatures:

☐ Dryad

☐ Ghost

☐ Sphinx

☐ The Great Booga

☐ Ebony Elephant

☐ Merlin, the robot owl

☐ Chupacabra

☐ Robot Crab

☐ Prized Porker

☐ Other: _____

Shark Fins

Trash

Pick three locations:

☐ Land of the Purple Giant

☐ DaVinci's Workshop

☐ Poseidon's Kingdom

☐ The Moon

☐ Dragon Cove

☐ Sully's Steam-Powered Paraphernalia

☐ Comic Shop

☐ Booga Bay

☐ The Dark Forest

☐ Count Bram's Castle

☐ Karaoke Bar

☐ The Cemetery

☐ Jungle Planet

☐ Other: _____

Pick two items:

- ☐ Bolt cutters
- ☐ Flashlight
- ☐ Binoculars
- ☐ RC helicopter
- ☐ Toolbox
- ☐ Crossbow
- ☐ Mandrake root
- ☐ Fishing pole
- ☐ Chameleon suit
- ☐ Digital camera
- ☐ Shovel
- ☐ Rope
- ☐ Reed pipe
- ☐ Shrinking soda
- ☐ Other: _____

SO WHAT DID YOU THINK OF THIS BOOK?

☐ Awesome

☐ Really awesome

☐ Super awesome

☐ Extra-super awesome

☐ Other: _____

Hey, you made it to the end! No more quizzes. Instead, here are some mini-posters you can cut out and hang up.